For Dimitri, an inquiring mind
—JD & DS

Agent Lion and the Case of the Missing Party
Copyright © 2021 by Jacky Davis and David Soman
All rights reserved. Manufactured in Italy.
www.harpercollinschildrens.com

ISBN 978-0-06-286918-0

The artist used pen and ink and watercolor to create the illustrations for this book.
Typography by Chelsea C. Donaldson
20 21 22 23 24   RTLO   10 9 8 7 6 5 4 3 2 1
❖
First Edition

AGENT LION

and the Case of the Missing Party

DAVID SOMAN AND JACKY DAVIS

HARPER

An Imprint of HarperCollinsPublishers

Agent Lion was hard at work..

Suddenly his secret radio buzzed!

It was a message from headquarters:

He had to get to the Hotel Du Lox right away
to help Petunia Skunk find her

missing birthday party!

Agent Lion arrived at the hotel and went
directly to the front desk.

Ding, ding, ding, ding, ding!

"May I help you, sir?" said Mr. Koala.

"Yes! Would you please hold this?"
asked Agent Lion.

"There you are, Agent Lion!" said Petunia. "My birthday cake and all the decorations have gone missing from the party room. I need you to help me find my party."

Blink
Blink
Blink

Petunia led him to the scene
of the disappearance.

"The party was all set up in this very room," Petunia told Agent Lion. "And now everything is gone!"

"Let's begin the investigation," declared Agent Lion. "Aha! A witness. Tell me, have you seen any suspicious activity around here?"

"Look," called Petunia. "There are chocolate-frosting paw prints on this doorknob!"

"Hmm, chocolate frosting?" Agent Lion said. "Don't you think strawberry frosting is better?"

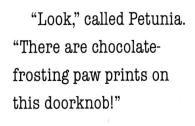

"What? No, Agent Lion!" said Petunia. "Come on! Whoever took my cake probably went through this door!"

"Perhaps they were looking for strawberry frosting," suggested Agent Lion.

In the hall, they saw a bellhop and Ms. Walrus waiting for an elevator.

"Just one minute!" said Agent Lion. "What are all those suspiciously wrapped packages?"

"Pish! Posh!" sniffed Ms. Walrus. "That is my luggage!"

"Or is it?" accused Agent Lion.

"It is," replied Ms. Walrus. "And that is my hat, sir."

"Hurry, Agent Lion!" cried Petunia. "That looks like
the cart that my cake was on, and it's getting away!"

Agent Lion and Petunia chased after the cart and ran into the Hotel Du Lox dining room.

"There you are!" charged Agent Lion. "We have found you, **party thief!**"

But the waiter was only serving Mr. Turtle's lettuce soup.

"Then 'lettuce' leave you to your soup," giggled Agent Lion. "Get it?"

"Enjoy your soup, Mr. Turtle!" said Petunia.

As they continued their search, Agent Lion noticed something peculiar.

"Hmm," he said.

"What is it?" asked Petunia.

"Why would someone just leave a party streamer on the floor?" he asked.

"Agent Lion, that's a clue from my party! And it leads to that set of doors."

Agent Lion and Petunia pushed open the doors . . .

. . . and quickly closed them.

"Perhaps we should continue our search somewhere else?" said Petunia.

"Good idea," replied Agent Lion.

They decided to investigate the swimming pool area.

"I will show you how I do the lion paddle," said Agent Lion.

"Pardon me, have you seen a missing birthday party?"
Agent Lion inquired.

Boing! Boing! Boing!

At the edge of the pool, Petunia discovered more clues.
"We should follow the trail of party favors!" she said.

"Okay!" agreed Agent Lion. "But first
I must investigate the slide at least
three more times!"

Agent Lion and Petunia dried off and followed the clues that led them down a hallway,

around a corner,

and another corner,
until . . .
they came to a
closed door.

"It is dark inside," whispered Agent Lion.
"So I will go first."

Inside there was a **loud crash** and a muffled yell.
Petunia dashed into the room and turned on the lights.
"Agent Lion, are you okay?" she asked.

"Of course," he said. "And I have found this mop!"

"A mop is *not* a clue," replied Petunia.

"True," said Agent Lion. "But it is very good for mopping!"

"Agent Lion," said Petunia, "we are out of clues. How will we ever find my missing birthday party?"

"Don't worry, Petunia!" Agent Lion reassured her. "We'll find your party. Maybe we just to need to take a break. Sometimes I do my best thinking when I'm not thinking."

They took a moment to do some not-thinking.

"Look at the pretty balloon," said Agent Lion. "It reminds me of a movie I once saw that involved a young cub in Paris."

"Agent Lion, that isn't just a balloon," said Petunia. "It's the clue that we've been looking for!"

Agent Lion and Petunia got up and raced after the balloon, and then they saw another, and then another.

"They're coming from behind these doors!" announced Petunia.

Petunia pushed open the door, and everyone shouted,

Happy Birthday!

"How did the party get *here*?" asked Petunia.

"Madam," explained Mr. Koala, "we apologize for moving the party. It had simply become too large for the other room. We hope you weren't too inconvenienced."

"Actually, it was fun to search for my party," admitted Petunia.

"It is said," added Ms. Walrus, "that the journey matters more than the destination."

"Excellent detective work, Petunia!" said Agent

Lion. "We found your party even though the hotel tried to hide it from us. This magnifying glass is your birthday present, because we are a fantastic team!"